Chinook Christmas

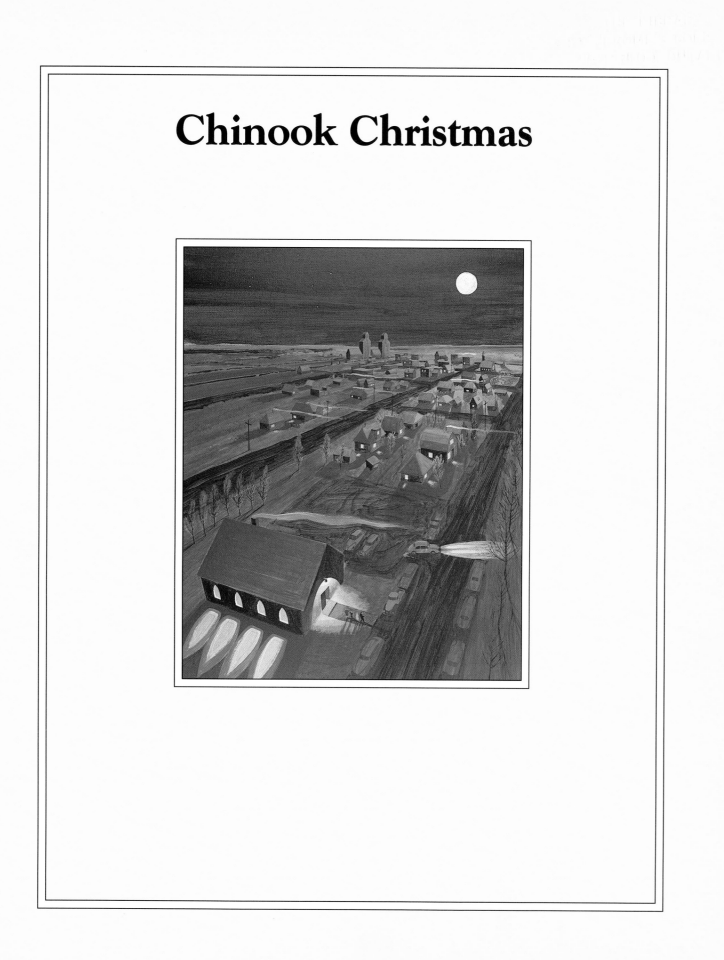

NORTHERN LIGHTS BOOKS FOR CHILDREN ARE PUBLISHED BY
Red Deer College Press
56 Avenue & 32 Street Box 5005
Red Deer Alberta Canada T4N 5H5

ACKNOWLEDGEMENTS
Printed and bound in Canada by D.W. Friesen Ltd. for Red Deer College Press.
The publishers gratefully acknowledge the financial assistance of the Alberta Foundation for the Arts, Alberta Culture & Multiculturalism, The Canada Council, Red Deer College, and Radio 7 CKRD.

CANADIAN CATALOGUING IN PUBLICATION DATA
Wiebe, Rudy, 1934–
Chinook Christmas
(Northern Lights Books for Children)
ISBN 0-88995-086-5
I. More, David. II. Title. III. Series.
PS8545.I38C5 1992 jC813'.54 C92-091324-5
PZ7.W53Ch 1992

Chinook Christmas

Story by Rudy Wiebe
Paintings by David More

NORTHERN LIGHTS BOOKS FOR CHILDREN

Red Deer College Press

THE WINTER I turned nine was our first in southern Alberta, and the snowy scars of irrigation ditches circling lower and lower into the long, shallow hollow of our town seemed to me then like the trenches of some besieging army. The grey, wrinkled snow lay driven there off the tilted fields, long, long welts of it carved in parallels below the square top of Big Chief Mountain sixty miles away where the implacable General of the Winds stood forever roaring at his troops: *Advance!*

Relentless west wind, roaring in my head all fall, the cottonwoods bent so low east that one day I straightened up on the pedals of my bicycle and discovered I could stand motionless, balanced, the wind's weight a wall, a power that held me shivering uneasily facing into it.

But then I was nudged, clubbed, and I let the wind wheel me round like always and I spread my arms akimbo, my jacket held wide at the waist, and went no hands sailing along the gravel street, through three ridged stop-corners on the fly to Jakie's house. I leaned into his yard like a racing sloop, all canvas spread, and met him wobbling forward on his bike beside the little irrigation ditch that was filling their cistern for winter so I knocked him into that grey water, and then he knocked me into it too.

"Let's ride to the main ditch," Jakie said, trying to blink through the mud in his eyes.

"Sure," I said. "We'll get it anyways, we might as well get it good."

He was three years older than I, and that summer we had become uneasy friends with the town's whole length of one-way wind between us. Because we were second cousins (twice removed at that, my father said, but for Mennonites scattered around Canada that meant a lot then), and mostly because neither of us had any other friends. And because of Anni. My sister Anni always knew what she wanted.

"We have to have a Christmas tree," Anni said. "How'll we ever find one here, nothing but sugar beet fields and ditches?"

She was fourteen. The spring before, when we left our bush homestead up north so my father could work on an irrigation dairy and Mama and Anni and I could thin beets, she had already been kissed once or twice under a full moon. She still thought that a good deal better than getting sunburned between endless beet rows, wrinkling up, hunched over like every other poor woman and child she saw stoop-shouldered in every southern field.

Up north she and I always ploughed our Christmas tree out of the muskeg, our dog bounding high through soft cushions of snow, the air so motionless between the muskeg spruce—flounced, layered, and blazing white with brown and green edges.

"There's a tree on old Heidebrecht's front lawn," I said. "It's real pretty."

"Oh sure," and Anni sang,

"Chop chop hoo–ra–a–a–il,

Christmas in ja–a–a–il,

How can we fa–a–a–il,

They will throw out our heads in a pa–a–a–il."

"Anyways," I told her, "a Christmas tree isn't even Christian. It's heathen."

Old Ema Racht—Old "Always Right" (but in Low German it rhymes, Ema R*a*cht Heidebr*a*cht)—had the biggest Mennonite house in town. He had sold his farm to one of his sons for an unbelievable price (that was what he was mostly right about: buying low and selling very high), and now he drove a black Buick to church twice every Sunday with his ancient daughter as stiff and erect as himself beside him. He always roared the engine until he could see a cloud of bluish smoke through the rear window, then he slowly let out the clutch and began to move, shoving in the clutch a little as soon as the car threatened to go too quickly but never taking his foot off the gas. All summer his lawn, shaded by giant cottonwoods and blue-coned spruce, was bright green like a frog's belly.

"A Christmas tree's heathen? Who said, smarty head?" Anni twirled around me.

"In Sunday school, Mr. Rempel," I said. He was tall with broad shoulders and had "adorable," Anni had once confessed, curly blonde hair.

That stopped her—for two seconds. But I saw immediately it was astonishment at my still holding such an out-dated opinion that was spreading like a cat's tongue licking over her face. She laughed aloud.

"He's no fun," she said irrelevantly. "In fact, he's kinda dumb."

"How do you know?" I hit her with anything I could think of: "You've never even *talked* to him."

"He's a curly blonde," Anni threw over her shoulder, going into the kitchen. I never had enough for her, of anything.

Ohhhhhh, the kitchen before Christmas! A whole pasture of smells gone crazy in spring, not only from two kinds of cookies—oatmeal with one chocolate chip topping each, and pale almost brownly bluish shapes of ammonia creatures Mama had let me stamp out of thick dough—but also cinnamon rolls with their bottoms up, exuding sweet brown syrup and dimpled raisins like twirled targets to aim an uncontrollable finger at—

"Mama! Eric's poking the rolls!"

—and tiny square *pyrushkis* with their tops folded up into peaked and quartered little tents of ridged, golden crust that oozed juices, red strawberry and royal purple saskatoon and pale, creamy apple, how for the love of Christmas and stomach could anyone keep their hands off—

"Eric!"

And outside was chinook.

The evening before a long bow of golden light had grown along the western horizon under the ceiling of clouds hammered down overhead solid as rafters. At the end of the day, the grey monolith of Big Chief Mountain sat for a moment exposed against blue and that golden streak, like a knife tip about to slit open the rest of the horizon, with a faint smell of crushed, irrigated clover in summer slipping through to wander over the glazed drifts. And also—a touch of warmth; very nearly a flare of mad possibility in the cold. Today, it all blazed into actuality, my head huge as if its bones were unhinged, spread open for me to breathe that clover without sniffing after it, all the air burning with it, the drifts already wrinkling down into sodden sponges and the air swimming limpid like creek water on a May morning. Chinook!

It fondled my bare head and our chickens sang behind their tiny windows. I opened the barn door, and their acrid, avian mist was swallowed whole, disappeared into the morning brilliance of chinook. Our white-faced cow lifted her head above the dry alfalfa of her manger, her ears gesturing gently as they did whenever she was moved to ponderous, liquid-eyed, and bovine contentment. Go on Boss, you bulgy hay-chewer, your warm flanks to butt my head against, your long, soft teats swishing hot milk between my rhythmic fingers—go on, you globed, warm femaleness and breathe all that spring, that momentary, maddening spring the day before Christmas.

"There are still some trees left, Mrs. Orleski on her lot," I said, shifting the basket of *Zwieback* to my other arm.

Anni carried two pails of layered pastry for Tante Tien, and though they were heavier, they were actually easier to carry because she could walk balanced. The basket in the basket of my bike would have been best, but the chinook had only licked the gravel street dry in blotches and left the rest wet, water running everywhere under the snow-levelled ditches. It was everywhere slurp and slide and temptation to not catch your balance before you tucked your head and rolled soft and squitchy and came up all over coated with three-times gumbo like your laden boots.

"She told us," Anni said. "A tree costs at least a dollar."

"Yeah, the miserblist one, we'd never—"

"That's no word, 'miserblist.'"

"Miser-*er*bilist?"

"Miser-*erb*alist, rhymes with 'herb-*a*list,'" Anni sang, skipping a puddle too nonchalantly perhaps and slipping beautifully, but sliding herself into balance so that only her left pail bottom came up small gravel and heavy heavy gumbo. We wiped it off with snow, left the food in Tante Tien's barren kitchen with her small horde of children rolling their small, barbarian eyes at the steamy warmth of things, and ran out before the small, barbarian fingers could—

"Eric and I have to get back because Mama needs us and Father is coming home right after supper and the church . . . ."

Anni hauled me out with her long arm and swinging, muddy pail and there was Jakie, leaning against the cottonwood in the front yard. Looking absolutely Chicago gangster to the very bend of his leg and cap pulled tight over his eyes.

"If you want a tree so bad," he said, "why don't you take it?"

Anni actually stopped and looked at him. Chinooks touch everyone differently: all he needed was a short machine gun.

"There's never nobody there at night," he said.

It was very hard to read Anni's expression, and Jakie must have made the same mistake I made because he continued, still looking at his fingernails which were very long and smooth with nice moons at their base.

"Anyways, who'd miss one shitty little tree?"

"I presume," Annie said—and her tone warned me instantly—"I presume that if there is *never nobody* there, there must *always* be *somebody*, and I presume further that not even an habitual criminal would be so stupid as to steal under such conditions, leave alone someone honest at Christmas when a chinook is blowing."

Her statement would have been stronger without mentioning either Christmas or chinook, and I think Anni felt so too because we hadn't left Jakie more than half a block behind, still leaning against the tree and studying the perfect moons of his fingernails, when she inexplicably commented,

"He won't even get as far as his stupid dad, he'll just end up in jail."

"What's the matter with Oncle Willm?" I asked.

To tell the truth, I liked Oncle Willm. He was certainly the strongest man in town, not much taller than I but so broad he walked sideways through any door, and he could place his thick arms under half a frozen beef and hoist it around and up onto a hook in one immense motion without breathing hard or slipping on the sawdust under his butcher's chopping block. Unlike any other Mennonite grown-up, he cracked jokes with me, and so did Mrs. Cartwright who sold the meat for him.

Mrs. Cartwright was always dressed so perfectly, her face as careful as a picture, and when she leaned over the counter, laughing, I always wanted to laugh with her, like every man who bought meat there did—though I never saw a woman do it—her lips and teeth so red and white and marvelously, smoothly exact. She laughed like no woman I had ever seen, deeply, powerfully, her entire vivid body pushing itself out at me and moving with it until I felt tight and awkward, somehow—inexplicably then—embarrassed.

"He's *not* our uncle, thank Jehoshaphat," Anni snapped, and then seeing me goggle-eyed, said quickly, "There's Mr. Ireland, let's catch a ride!"

Mr. Ireland's dray with its unmatched greys was moving toward the Canadian Pacific Railway station in the evening shadow of the elevators, but it seemed that in any case Anni had intended not to go directly home, but rather "downtown" as we called it. (Our town had three parallel streets south of the railway tracks and three north, with avenues at right angles numbered 100 at the centre, and higher and lower on either side in anticipation of more or less measureless and endless growth.) So we hopped aboard the wagon and bounced along, dangling our legs off the tailgate.

The horses trotted while Mr. Ireland sang, the biggest grey plopping out hot, steamy buns, and Mr. Ireland interrupted himself to mutter, "Enough time for that later, Jock, get on with you!" He slapped the mountainous rear gently with a flat rein, and the buns appeared behind the wagon under us in perfect single-file pattern like a queue of smooth-headed children, steaming slightly as they sank out of sight in the gumbo. The chinook blustered violently through trees and over a roof, and suddenly Mr. Ireland began to roar with it as we passed the Japanese Buddhist church that was swallowing a snake of small brown children I knew—

"Oh, he shot her through the window,
And the bullet's in her yet!"

—and the dray sighed silently across Main Street at 101 Avenue on its fat balloon tires salvaged from World War II fighter planes. A huge, black truck with its grain box standing tight full of Hutterites, beards and polka-dotted kerchiefs facing into the wind, rolled past and squitched a grey pothole of mud at us, but missed.

"Do men have yets too?" I asked Anni.

"Yets?"

"He sang, 'The bullet's in her yet.'"

Anni laughed. "No," she spluttered, "only women. And you have to shoot them through their windows to hit their yets!"

But then, still laughing, she knocked one of our pails off, and we had to jump anyways because we were passing the high front of the largest grocery and hardware store, Doerksen Bros. Props., and that's where Mrs. Orleski had her Christmas trees leaning against the wall.

Mrs. Orleski usually sold *Lethbridge Herald*s at the corner for a nickel, perhaps two or three a day since Hermie Kudreck had the town sewed up with home delivery (Hermie owned a CCM three-speed by the time he was ten, a Harley Davidson at fifteen, and an Olds convertible at nineteen, all starting from *Herald* saturation of our town), but when the Doerksen Brothers started playing Christmas carols on the gramophone at the back of their store, she shifted to the vacant lot. One day it was white, bare, the next heavy green, thick with needled aroma like the mountains where Mrs. Orleski said her son worked deep in the Crowsnest Mines.

I could not imagine that then. Crows' nests were bundles of sticks notched high in poplars and a coal mine was . . . what? When her son came home for one day at Christmas, you could see the coal dust engrained in his skin, like topsoil in the drifts of a three-day prairie blizzard. His shoulders had a hockey player's powerful slope and were only a little narrower than Oncle Willm's, and he liked to show his favourite muscle, a bulge when he bent his elbow that heaved up and clenched itself rock hard. Not even Whipper Billy Watson, the heavyweight wrestling champion of the world, could muster that, he said. He knew because he had once challenged Watson to show, and that dead-white mound of muscle from Toronto had backed off: nothing but the usual stuff in his arm.

"Jolly old St. Nicholas, lean your ear this way.

Don't you tell a single soul . . ."

murmured the wall of the store. If the Doerksen Brothers leaned any farther, Anni said, they would fall over.

"You kits still lookin'?" Mrs. Orleski pulled her hands from between her three summer coats and whatever else she wore underneath, sweaters and skirts and every kind of unmentionable. "Sell, lotsa sell this year, see," and she gestured around with her arms wide, a thick little stump turning as if about to break into dance.

There were only three trees left, three scrunchy trees in a trampled scatter of spruce tips and sodden snow. And abruptly she wheeled: her nostrils flared into the chinook, opening huge like gills in fast water.

"Here, here! They leave it, the leetle branch, they leave it lotsa . . . " and she was stooping, gathering with the swift, inevitable hands of workers, "Sometimes stump, have it too much branch . . . . "

And she thrust them at me. Offering in the wimpling eddy of the sun-and-wind-warmed wall a stinging memory of motionless, feathered muskeg, our black dog plunging head and tail through the crystalline velvet sinking of it, the indented spoors of rabbits and a slither of weasels: Mrs. Orleski's two stubby arms filled with spruce boughs like a proffered squirrel's nest stuffed fat and full and warm for the winter,

"You take it, is good, hang it some places, Mama happy, so . . . . "

Offering the wistful, windy madness of a gift.

Anni said, "I'm sorry," and I stared at her in horror. "We still have no money."

"Wha? I no take it, your money . . . give for nutting. You . . . take!"

And I took and ran. Anni behind me argued, the very bend of her body declaring that she could not accept a gift from someone as poor as herself and certainly not from anyone richer, and so she refused to accept anything from anyone, ever; and finally thanked the old lady almost angrily, as if forced. And followed me, her long legs scissoring through the last sunshine, past the Principal's yellow and green house, and across the school yard. The little oriental houses stood one by one along the south side of the street, their double windows with their pale, never-opened blinds dreaming through the long winter like unfathomable Buddhas.

"It's Christmas, and anyway it cleans up her lot."

But any word of mine just set Anni's teeth more visibly into her bottom lip, her head lower into the branches as if she would chew needles. Both her pails were stuck full, and my basket was too small for all my armful, but I didn't drop a twig all the way home, and I slid neither flat nor flying in the mud either.

Old Ema Racht passed us, alone like a procession in his smoking Buick. In the rich darkness of the car his whiskers flared from the sides of his face like white flames reaching for the side windows as he drove without headlights, his arms braced rigid before him, and his eyes peering ahead as if to illuminate the fluid road with their glare. The chinook seeped spruce through my head. Had I known about such things then, I would have known I was at least drunk when I heaved up my branches, waved, shouted, *Frohe Wiehnachte!* ("HAPPY CHRISTMAS!")

And his head turned around to us, trudging the shoulder of the road, turned heavily around like a row of cannon wheeling.

And he saw me, his eyes briefly the driven ends of spikes, and the huge, polished flank of the car lurched toward me as at a recognition before his head trundled back and cocked forward again on his long neck over the steering wheel and his stiff arms kept his shoulders rammed back against the seat and his beaked nose defied that lunatic wind, dared it to squirm him into the gumbo ditch: he would *not* turn that wheel, he would *not* raise either his right foot from the gas or his left foot from the clutch.

And so he roared away into the warm, settling dusk of Christmas Eve, finally merging far ahead of us into the misty dinosaur legs of the cottonwoods surrounding his immense yard: an antediluvian monster roaring in futile anthem the cacophonous wonders of the Christ-child season. Gifts upon gifts, the smell of gas and clutchplate snipped at our nostrils through the green of spruce till we saw the rectangular windows of our house stunned golden every one with the vanished sun reflecting from the laden, burning bellies of the clouds, and the mud squishing under our feet and the prick of spruce on our cold wrists and fingers. I looked at Anni.

Her hair streamed flat under wind, the cloven flames of window and sky glistened, blazed in her eyes.

"Don't say a word," she said.

And I did that. Even when I saw our father was already home because the dairy pick-up was parked outside our door, I said nothing. But once inside, ohhhhh, talk! Our house was packed tight with smells like nuts in a Christmas cake, and we hung our branches singing everywhere until its two rooms seemed flung all over with a green and poignant spray. Then we stepped into the fresh darkness and the purring, dialed cab of the truck wafted us to church.

A wide building, where the men sat in two broad aisles on the right and the women in two aisles on the left and we children crammed in front, directly under the benign (for tonight) faces of the aged ministers leaning over the pulpit and the choir curved around behind them. We sang those Christmas songs our people had brought from half a world away, so out of place now in the treeless, flat irrigation prairies, but not at all out of spirit:

Leise rieselt der Schnee,

(LIGHTLY FALLETH THE SNOW,)

Still und starr ruht der See;

(STILL AND WHITE RESTS THE SEA;)

Weihnachtlich glänzet der Wald,

(WOODS GLISTEN UNDER THE MOON,)

Freuet Euch, Christkind kommt bald!

(JOY TO THEE, CHRISTCHILD COMES SOON!)

—the high, beautiful voices of the women, the deep, heavy voices of the men, and the bright thread of my father's tenor between them, where he sat behind me among rich farmers and storekeepers and workers and teachers and unemployed labourers. Two ministers spoke, very short and mostly stories, and there were several long prayers and the choir sang, several children's groups sang, and then we all sang again,

> *Nun ist sie erschienen,*
>
> *die himmlische Sonne . . .*
>
> (THE SUN HAS ARISEN IN HEAVENLY GLORY . . .)

and

> *O Fest aller heiligen Feste,*
>
> (HAIL HEAVENLY NIGHT, O MOST HOLY,)
>
> *O Weihnacht, du lieblicher Schein . . .*
>
> (O CHRISTMAS, HOW LOVELY THOU ART . . .)

—and then young men came in with big boxes and gave every child a small, brown bag which we were not allowed to open in church, but we could so easily feel whether we had an orange or an apple, and there was at least one chocolate bar and almost a whole handful of peanuts and maybe even six or seven candies, and then we sang in whatever language we liked,

Stille Nacht, heilige Nacht,
(SILENT NIGHT, HOLY NIGHT,)
Alles schläft, einsam wacht
(ALL IS CALM, ALL IS BRIGHT)
Nur das traute, hochheilige Paar,
(ROUND YON VIRGIN MOTHER AND CHILD,)
Holder Knabe im Lockigen Haar
(HOLY INFANT SO TENDER AND MILD)
Schlaf in himmlischer Ruh',
(SLEEP IN HEAVENLY PEACE,)
Schlaf in himmlischer Ruh'.
(SLEEP IN HEAVENLY PEACE.)

And then without talking or running around, we all went quickly and quietly home.

No clouds now, the sky was brilliant, clear black with crystals of stars frozen over us, the air silent as a curtain: tomorrow would be very cold. And on our front step, a small wooden box. I bumped against it as I jumped for the door, trying to get in fast to see whether I had an O Henry or a Sweet Marie in my bag.

The board squeaked up—what was that?

"Those are oranges," my father said. "Japanese oranges. They can be eaten."

Roundly moist in their pale wrappers, they unzipped themselves under his fingernail symmetrically with a strange, sharp sweetness like regular little oriental shelves opening. Who could have left them for us? Such a vividly useless gift, all you could do was eat it. So we did. Anni and I each ate nine.

Then my father read, as he always did, from "And there went out a decree from Caesar Augustus . . ." all the way to where the shepherds returned to their flocks, glorifying and praising God, and then we each said a very short prayer with the house so quiet now that I could hear the coal shift as it burned in the stove, and Anni and I placed our plates—like always, the very biggest we could find—on the kitchen table under the spruce branches, all ready for the gifts we knew we would get from the "Nate Klous" (always useful gifts like toothbrushes or socks or a shirt at most), and then we climbed up the narrow stairs to our two small rooms with a final, tenth, japanese shelving itself lingeringly into our mouths.

Anni asked, "Who was it?" breathing orange in the darkness.

I said, "Who knows?"

But I did. I knew it as certainly as a child knows everything at Christmas. As certainly as the hard, clear sanity of the North Wind's song beginning at the window, and in my ear, our little house I believe swaying gently like a cradle, very, very gently.